Enid Blyton
Bedtime Stories

This edition first published in the United Kingdom in 1999 by
Brockhampton Press
20 Bloomsbury Street
London WC1B 3QA
a member of the Hodder Headline PLC Group

© Text copyright, Enid Blyton Limited
© Illustration copyright, Hodder and Stoughton Limited

Designed and produced for Brockhampton Press by
Open Door Limited
80 High Street, Colsterworth, Lincolnshire NG33 5JA

Colour separation: GA Graphics Stamford
Printed in Singapore

Title: Enid Blyton Bedtime Stories
ISBN: 1-84186-001-8

Enid Blyton
Bedtime Stories

BROCKHAMPTON PRESS

Contents

Contents

The Birds and the Bun

There was once a baker's boy who went down Leafy Lane with a basket of bread and buns. As he went he sang a song and swung his basket, and out dropped a bag with a large currant bun inside. The boy did not see the bun falling and he went on his way. The bun lay in the lane in its paper bag, and as no one came by that way it stayed there for a whole hour.

Then a robin came by and saw it. "A paper bag, a paper bag!" he cried.

A brown sparrow flew down and pecked at the bag. "There's something inside!" he chirrupped.

Down flew a fine chaffinch and pecked open the bag. "I have pecked a hole!" he sang, "I have pecked a hole!"

Then a big blackbird fluttered down and put his head inside the hole. "There is a bun inside!" he sang. "A bun, a big currant bun!"

A thrush joined the little crowd and he pecked at the bun. "It is good!" he said. "I shall eat it. It is mine."

"Yours!" cried the robin, indignantly. "What do you mean? I saw the paper bag first!"

"But I told you there was something inside the bag!" chirrupped the sparrow, at once. "I did, I did!"

The chaffinch pushed against the thrush. "Go away!" He cried. "This is my bun. It was I who pecked a hole in the bag."

"But I peeped inside it!" said the blackbird. "The bun is mine. Go away, everybody!"

"You are foolish!" said the thrush, scornfully. "I pecked the bun first – so it is mine. I am now going to eat it!"

Then there was such a noise of quarrelling and chirrupping and singing that no one could hear himself speak. Suddenly there was a large caw and down flew a large black rook.

"What is the matter?" he said, in his deep voice.

Then everyone told him about the bun in the paper bag.

"And each of us thinks it is his," said the thrush. "How can we settle it?"

"I will settle it for you," said the rook. "Now, you all have good voices, I will hear you sing for this bun, and I will give it to the one who sings the best."

"That is a good idea," cried everyone, for they all thought they had fine voices, even the shrill sparrows.

"Very well," said the rook. "Now please turn round so that you have your backs to me. When I say 'Go!' open your beaks and sing loudly for all you are worth, till I say stop."

So the robin, the sparrow, the chaffinch, the thrush and the blackbird all turned round with their backs to the rook, opened their beaks, and waited for him to say "Go!"

"Go!" he shouted. And then you should have heard the robin's creamy trill, the sparrow's loud chirrup, the chaffinch's pretty rattle of a song, the thrush's lovely notes and the blackbird's fluting. Really, it was fine to hear. They went on and on and on – and they didn't hear the rook tearing open the paper bag. They didn't hear him taking out the bun. They didn't hear him spreading his great black wings and flying off into the next field. No, they went on and on singing, each trying to outsing the rest.

When they were quite tired of singing, they wondered why the rook did not tell them to stop. So the robin looked round – and he saw that the rook was gone!

He hopped over to the paper bag – and it was empty!

"See, see!" he cried. "The bun is gone – and so is the rook! He has tricked us! Oh, the rascal! Oh, the scamp! Now we have lost our bun!"

"And there was plenty there for all of us!" chirrupped the sparrow, in dismay. "Why did we make such a fuss? We could each have had some – and now we have none!"

They flew off in a rage – and you may be sure the rook didn't show himself for a day or two! And when he did, and happened to meet the others, he cawed politely, and said: "Really, my friends, you have REMARKABLY fine singing voices! Do let me hear you some other time!"

And you should hear them shout at him then!

A Basket of Surprises

When Jimmy's mother went to the Garden Fair at the Vicarage she brought a very beautiful basket. It was large and round and deep, and had a fine, strong handle. All round the basket was a pretty green and yellow pattern. It really was a very fine basket, and Jimmy's mother was pleased with it.

"Now, you are not to borrow this basket for anything, Jimmy," she said to him. "You can have my old one if you want one. This is to be kept for special things, like taking eggs to Granny, or something like that."

Jimmy promised. He was once allowed to take some flowers in the basket to old Mr. White, but that was all. And then one day he wanted a basket to take his trains, signals and lines to his friend's, Billy Brown. He went to find the old basket and it wasn't there. His mother was out and no one was at home except Tibby, the big tabby cat, sitting by the fire.

"Where's the old basket, Tibby?" Jimmy asked her, but she just mewed and sat on by the fire, thinking her pussy thoughts. Jimmy hunted everywhere. There was no old basket to be found at all. Perhaps his mother had taken it.

"Well, I'll have to take the new basket," said Jimmy. "I can't possibly take all my things without a basket."

So he took down the beautiful new basket and packed his things into it.

Then off he went to Billy's and had a fine tea and a fine game. Billy begged him to lend him his railway for a day, so Jimmy said he would. He set off home with the empty basket, swinging it by the big handle.

He had to go through the woods on his way home, and as he ran he saw a bird fly into a bush. "Hello!" thought Jimmy. "There's a nest there. I'll just peep and see. I won't disturb the bird in case it deserts its nest – but I would just like to see if there are any baby birds there."

He pushed his way into the bush, but the bird flew out again and into another bush. Jimmy followed her. He felt sure she must have a nest somewhere. But she hadn't. She was just looking for the caterpillars there.

Jimmy set off home again – but suddenly he remembered that he had put down his basket somewhere. Goodness! Where could it be?

He ran back – but no matter how he looked he couldn't find that basket anywhere! "Oh, dear!" thought Jimmy, as he hunted. "Whatever will Mummy say if I go home without it? I am sure I put it down by the bush I first looked in."

But Jimmy couldn't find the bush! And at last he had to go home without the basket. When he told his mother he had lost it she was very cross.

"You are a naughty boy, Jimmy," she said. "I told you not to borrow my best basket. Now, unless it is found again, you must save up your money and buy me a new one."

"Oh, but Mummy, I'm saving up to buy a railway tunnel!" cried Jimmy, in dismay.

"Well, I'm sorry, dear, but you can't buy your tunnel until you have bought a new basket," said his mother. "You had better go and have another hunt for it."

Poor Jimmy! He went and hunted and hunted, but he could not find that basket! The next day his Uncle Peter came to see him and gave him some money to spend – but his mother said to put it all in his money-box to save up for the new basket. He was dreadfully disappointed. The next morning his mother called him and said: "Have you seen Tibby, Jimmy? She isn't in her usual place by the fire, and she hasn't been in for her breakfast."

"No, I haven't seen her," said Jimmy quite worried, for he was very fond of Tibby. "Where can she be?"

"Perhaps she will come in for her dinner," said his mother. But Tibby didn't. There was no sign of her at all. Jimmy got more and more worried. He had had Tibby from a kitten, and the two were great friends. He did so hope she hadn't got caught in a trap.

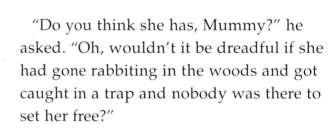

"Do you think she has, Mummy?" he asked. "Oh, wouldn't it be dreadful if she had gone rabbiting in the woods and got caught in a trap and nobody was there to set her free?"

"Oh, I don't expect she has, for a moment," said his mother. "She hardly ever goes rabbiting. She will turn up, I expect. Now, what are you going to do this afternoon, Jimmy? You said you wanted to go and play with Billy Brown."

"Well, I did want to," said Jimmy. "But I think I'll just go and hunt for Tibby, Mummy, I do feel unhappy about her, really I do."

"After tea we will catch the bus and go into the town to buy a new basket," said his mother. "I really must have another. I think you have enough money in your box to buy me one."

Jimmy went off to hunt for Tibby, feeling very miserable. "I've lost Tibby, and I've got to give up my railway tunnel and buy a new basket instead," he sighed, as he ran along to the woods. "What a lot of bad luck all at once!"

He soon came to the woods, and he began hunting about, calling Tibby. He felt sure she must have been caught in a trap.

"Tibby, Tibby, Tibby!" he cried. "Where are you? Tibby, Tibby, Tibby!"

For some time he could hear nothing but the wind in the trees and the singing of the birds. Then he thought he heard a small mew.

"Tibby!" he shouted. "Tibby!"

"Miaow!" said a pussy-voice, and up ran Tibby to Jimmy, and purred and rubbed herself against his legs.

"Oh, dear Tibby!" said Jimmy, really delighted to see his cat again. He picked her up in his arms and made a fuss of her. She purred loudly, and then tried to get down.

"No, I'll carry you home, Tibby," said Jimmy, and he turned to go home. But Tibby struggled very hard,

and at last he had to let her go. She ran into the woods and disappeared. Jimmy was very much puzzled. He went after her.

"Tibby! Why don't you want to come home with me?" he called. "Come back! Where are you going?"

Tibby mewed from somewhere; then Jimmy saw her bright green eyes looking at him from a nearby bush! He ran up and knelt down to see where she was.

And, will you believe it, Tibby was lying comfortably down in the fine new basket that Jimmy had lost when he was looking for the bird's nest! There she was, as cosy as anything, looking up at Jimmy.

But there was still another surprise for the little boy for, when Tibby jumped out of the basket, what do you suppose he saw at the bottom? Why, five beautiful little Tabby kittens, all exactly like Tibby! He stared and stared and stared! He simply couldn't believe his eyes!

"Oh Tibby!" he said. "Oh Tibby! I've found you – and the basket – and some kittens too! Oh, whatever will Mummy say!"

He picked up the basket with the kittens and set off home. Tibby ran beside him mewing. When he got home he called his mother and showed her his surprising find.

She was just as astonished as he was! "Oh, Tibby, what darling little kittens!" she cried. "You shall have them in your own cosy basket by the fire! Fancy you finding our basket in the woods and putting your kittens there!"

"Mummy, I needn't spend my money on a new basket now, need I?" said Jimmy, pleased. "I can buy my tunnel with my money."

"Of course!" said his mother. "We will just put Tibby comfortably in her own basket with the kittens, and then we will catch the bus and go and buy your tunnel. You deserve it, really, Jimmy, because you gave up your afternoon's play with Billy to go and hunt for Tibby – and you found a basket of surprises, didn't you?"

So everyone was happy, and Jimmy got his railway tunnel after all. As for Tibby, she was very happy to be made such a fuss of, and you should have seen her kittens when they grew! They were the prettiest, dearest little things you could wish to see. I know, because, you see, I've got one of them for my own!

Tit for Tat

Jennifer, the curly-haired doll, had a little hairbrush of her own. She was very proud of it indeed, and the toys liked it, too, because it was fun to brush out Jennifer's lovely golden curls at night. Sometimes she lent it to the toys. Then the teddy bear brushed his short fur, the toy soldier brushed his bearskin hat, the pink cat brushed his coat and the clockwork mouse brushed his whiskers.

The little hairbrush lived in a small box with a little comb. Nobody used the comb because it was very small and it really wasn't any use for combing out Jennifer's thick curls. Sally, the little girl who owned all the toys, never bothered about the hairbrush at all. She hadn't brushed Jennifer's hair once with it, so it was a good thing the toys took turns at brushing it to make it look nice.

Then one day a most annoying thing happened. Sally was turning out her dolls' house and she wanted a brush to sweep the little carpets. She didn't want to borrow Mummy's brush because it was much too big for the tiny carpets.

So you can guess what she did. She borrowed Jennifer's little hairbrush. Just the thing!

"It's fine," said Sally, brushing away at the carpet. "Just right for this job. What a good thing I thought of it."

But the toys didn't think so at all! They looked on in dismay and Jennifer was almost in tears. Her own little hairbrush. How *mean* of Sally!

"Now I shan't be able to brush my hair with it any more," she thought. "It will be dirty and dusty and horrid. Oh, I do think Sally might have used something else. It's too bad of her."

Sally finished brushing the carpets and looked at the little brush. Such hard sweeping had almost worn it out.

"It's no use now," she said. "I'll throw it away." And into the fire it went! Oh, dear! The toys watched it blaze into flames for a minute or two – and then it was gone!

Jennifer, the curly-haired doll, cried that night. "I did like my little hairbrush," she said. "I've got such a lot of hair that I need a brush for it. Sally never brushes it for me. She doesn't look as if she brushes her own hair, either."

"She's an untidy little girl," said the bear. "She doesn't brush her teeth either. But she tells her mother that she does. She's a naughty story-teller."

"So she is," said the pink cat. "Do you know, her mother gave her a beautiful new green toothbrush last week and Sally hasn't used it yet? She hasn't cleaned her teeth all week."

"Then a toothbrush is just *wasted* on her!" said the clockwork mouse. "It's a pity we can't take it and use it to brush Jennifer's hair each night!"

"Dear me," said the bear, "that's a very fine idea, Mouse! Really very clever indeed. However did you think of it?"

The clockwork mouse would have blushed with delight at this praise if he could. "I don't know how I thought of it," he said. "I must be cleverer than I imagined."

"Shall we get Sally's toothbrush then?" said the pink cat. "I could climb up to the basin in the bathroom and reach up for it, I think. It's in her mug."

"All right. You go then," said the bear, and the pink cat went. He was quite good at jumping. He leapt up to the basin, slithered down into it, climbed up on to the shelf above, took Sally's perfectly new toothbrush in his mouth and jumped down to the floor again.

He padded into the playroom with it. The toys looked at it.

"The handle's too long," said the bear. "Much too long."

"Cut a bit off then," said the pink cat.

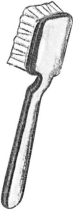

"What with?" asked the mouse.

"Sally's got some tools in a box," said Jennifer, the doll. "There's a little saw there. Couldn't we use that?"

Well, they could, of course, and they did! They found the little saw, and the bear sawed away valiantly at the handle of the toothbrush. Everyone watched in excitement.

The end of the handle suddenly fell off. The mouse picked up the little brush in delight. "Its handle is nice and short now," he said. "Just right for a hairbrush. Jennifer, do let me brush your hair for you."

So he was the first to brush the doll's curly hair with the new brush. It brushed beautifully because the bristles were harder than the ones in the hairbrush. Jennifer was delighted.

"Where shall we keep this brush?" asked the bear. "Better not put it into the box because Sally might see it."

"Put it into me," said the little tin teapot, in a spouty voice. "Sally never plays with me now. She'll never look inside me."

So that is where the toys keep the new hairbrush, in case you want to know.

The bear was a little bit worried at first. "Do you think we've done wrong to use Sally's toothbrush?" he said.

"Well, Sally took *my* brush and now we've taken hers, so it's tit for tat," said the curly-haired doll. "Anyway, she never used her toothbrush! We wouldn't have taken it if she did."

I'm just wondering what is going to happen when Sally's mother discovers that Sally's toothbrush is gone. It's going to be *very* difficult for naughty little Sally to make her mother believe that she is cleaning her teeth each night with a toothbrush that isn't there!

Holes in his Stockings

Mister Ho-Hhum was a brownie with twinkling eyes and a merry smile. He worked hard and was generous and good tempered – but there was just on thing he was always forgetting to do; and that was to mend the holes in his stockings.

His friend, Mister Hum-Hho, used to scold Ho-Hhum loudly, when he saw him taking off his shoes in the evening, and spied the enormous holes in the toes and heels of his stockings.

"Ho-Hhum!" he would cry. "Look at that dreadful hole, with your toe poking out! I'm ashamed of you. Why, don't you mend your stockings?"

"It doesn't matter," Ho-Hhum would say, with a grin. "Nobody sees them when I walk out. I don't take off my shoes in the street."

"Well, one day you *might* have to!" said Hum-Hho, "And then think how dreadful you would feel when everyone saw your toes poking through your stockings. I hope I'm not with you when *that* happens!"

"You needn't worry," said Ho-Hhum, gaily. "I shall NEVER take off my shoes in the street, so nobody will EVER see the holes in my stockings!"

And the naughty brownie went on wearing holey stockings every day – till something happened.

One Saturday morning he and Hum-Hho went out for a walk together, for it was a very fine day. They went round by the King's palace, and as they walked they heard the little Prince Peronel playing and shouting in the garden. Then suddenly they heard him cry bitterly.

The two brownies pushed open the garden door and rushed into the palace garden. They saw that the little Prince had tumbled out of his toy motor-car and had bumped his head One wheel was off the car and lay nearby on the ground.

Ho-Hhum picked up the little boy and wiped his tears. Hum-Hho picked up the motor car. Prince Peronel wept to see the wheel off.

"Now what shall I do?" he cried. "I can't ride in it!"

"If you've a hammer I could put the wheel on for you," said Ho-Hhum, kindly.

"I'm not allowed to have a hammer," said the little Prince. "But I know what you could do, brownie. Couldn't you take off your big, strong shoe and use that to knock my wheel on with? Oh, couldn't you?"

Mister Ho-Hhum thought he could quite well – and then, oh, my goodness me, he remembered that he had a great big hole in each of his stockings, and the holes would show dreadfully if he took his shoes off. Then what would the Prince think? He might even tell the King and Queen about the brownie that had holes in his stockings. So he shook his head.

"No," he said. "I can't use one of my shoes. I'll use a stone instead."

So he picked up a stone and tried to knock the wheel on with that. But the stone broke to pieces and a little bit flew off and cut the Prince's hand. He began to cry again and the two brownies were terribly upset.

"Why didn't you use your shoe as the Prince asked you?" said Hum-Hho to Ho-Hhum, quite forgetting that his friend had dreadful holes in his stockings. "Don't cry, little Prince. I'll knock the wheel on with one of *my* shoes!"

So Hum-Hho quickly slipped off one of his shoes and in a trice he had knocked the wheel on to the toy motor-car and mended it! Peronel was delighted.
He jumped in and rode down the path, calling loudly:

"Nurse! Mother! A kind brownie has mended my motor for me! Can he come to tea?"

Then, to the brownies' great surprise, who should come running down the path but the Fairy Queen herself, all in silver, shining like the moon. She kissed the little Prince and listened to what he had to say.

"I want this brownie to come to tea with me," he said, taking hold of Hum-Hho's hand. "Not the other one. He's unkind. He wouldn't take his shoe off and mend my wheel for me. But this one did."

Poor Ho-Hhum! He turned very red and ran out of the garden as fast as he could. As for Hum-Hho, he was so pleased at being asked for tea at the palace that he could hardly say a word! Off he went with the little Prince and had a lovely time. When he got home again, he called at Ho-Hhum's house to tell him about it.

And what was Ho-Hhum doing? Do you know? Of course you do! He was sitting on a stool, and round him were nine pairs of stockings, all with holes in – and Ho-Hhum was mending them as fast as he could.

"Don't scold me, Hum-Hho!" he cried, when he saw his friend. "I couldn't take my shoe off to mend the wheel because of the dreadful holes in my stocking. And now I am never going to have holey stockings again! Oh, how ashamed I felt to think I couldn't help the Prince!"

And two big tears rolled on to his darning-needle. Poor Ho-Hhum! Never mind, he has never had a hole in his stockings since that day!

The Sneezing Donkey

Once upon a time there was a small grey donkey who lived in a farm field and ate the grass and the thistles there. As he wandered across the field he felt a tickling in his nose. He lifted up his head and sneezed.

"A-tish-ee-aw!" he sneezed. "A-tish-ee-aw!"

His nose tickled again. He sneezed even more loudly. "A-TISH-ee-aw!"

He blinked and looked around. He could quite well feel another sneeze coming.

It came. "A-TISH-EE-TISH-EE-TISH-EE-AW!" he went, so loudly that some geese nearby fled away in alarm.

The donkey looked around, and to his surprise it had begun to pour with rain.

"That was my big sneeze did that," he thought to himself, pleased. "I have made it rain. I am really very clever. I shall tell everyone what I have done."

So he cantered over to the sheep and spoke to them. "Sheep, listen to me. Do you see this pouring rain? Well, I made it come when I sneezed so loudly!"

"How clever you are!" said the sheep admiringly. "Nothing happens when *we* sneeze!"

The donkey ran to the old brown horse and spoke to him, too. "Horse, listen to me. Do you see this pouring rain? Well, I made it come when I sneezed so loudly!"

"How clever you are!" said the horse admiringly. "Nothing happens when *I* sneeze!"

The donkey did feel proud. He wondered who else he could tell. He saw the hens and the cock at the end of the field and he trotted over to them. They were sheltering under the big hedge.

"Hens and cock, listen to me. Do you see this pouring rain? Well, I made it come when I sneezed so loudly!"

"How clever you are!" said the hens and cock admiringly. "Nothing happens when *we* sneeze – but thewn, we never *do* sneeze."

The donkey swung his long tail about, and wondered if he could tell anyone else. He saw the farm dog lying down in his tub and he cantered over to him.

"Rover, listen to me. Do you see this pouring rain? Well, I made it come by sneezing so loudly."

"How clever of you!" said Rover admiringly. "Nothing happens when *I* sneeze!"

The ducks came waddling by in a row, going to the pond. They were delighted with the rain. The donkey ran over to them.

"Ducks, listen to me," he said. "Do you see

this pouring rain? Well, *I* made it come when I sneezed so loudly."

"How clever of you!" said the ducks admiringly. "Nothing happens when *we* sneeze – but how we'd like it to rain whenever we sneeze!"

The donkey was so pleased with himself that he simply didn't know what to do.

The rain went on falling. It rained all day. It rained all night. It went on raining the next day too.

The sheep got tired of the rain. The brown horse got tired of the rain. The hens and the cock got tired of the rain. Rover got tired of the

rain. Everywhere was muddy. Everyone was wet and cold. Only the ducks liked the rain.

The sheep, the horse, the hens, cock and dog gathered together by the hedge and grumbled to one another.

"Look what that silly donkey has done with his sneezing! No one would have minded just a shower – but why should he make it rain all day and night like this? Let's go and tell him to stop the rain now."

So they went to the donkey. He was standing under a tree thinking how marvellous it was to have sneezed so much rain down.

"Donkey, we are wet and cold. Stop this rain at once," neighed the horse. "Donkey, our feathers are dripping. Stop this rain," clucked the hens and cock.

"Donkey, I have a feeling I shall bite your long tail if you don't sneeze again and *stop* the rain!" barked Rover, who could be very fierce.

The donkey stared at everyone in alarm. It had been easy enough to begin the rain – but he wasn't at all sure he could stop it. Besides, he couldn't sneeze unless a sneeze came. Whatever was he to do?

"The ducks like the rain," he said at last.

"If I stop the rain they will be angry and come and peck me."

"Well, we will be angrier and we will bite you, and nibble you and peck you too!" cried all the animals and birds at once.

"I don't know how to sneeze unless a sneeze happens to come," said the donkey, "and I don't know how to stop the rain."

"Well, why do you start a thing you don't know how to stop?" wuffed Rover crossly. "I shall snap at each of your legs!"

"And I shall butt you with my head," said the sheep.

"And I shall kick you with my heels," said the horse.

"And we will peck you with our beaks," said the birds. So they all began. They were so busy teasing the poor donkey that no one noticed that the clouds were blowing away – and the rain was stopping – and the sun was shining! But that was what was happening. The fields shone and glittered in the sun – it was a really lovely day.

"Stop! Stop!" cried the donkey. "Don't you see the sun?

Why are you teasing me like this? The rain has stopped! You ought to be ashamed of yourselves!" The animals and birds looked around. The donkey was right. It was a beautiful day. The rain had certainly stopped. They all went off joyfully and left the donkey alone in his corner of the field.

"Next time I sneeze I won't say anything about it" said the grey donkey. "Not a single word. There's no pleasing some people! They all said I was clever, too. Well, maybe I wasn't as clever as I thought I was!"

Next time he sneezed he was *so* surprised to find that no rain came. But *I'm* not surprised – are you?

The Toys Go to the Seaside

Once upon a time the goblin Peeko put his head in at the nursery and cried. "Who wants a day at the seaside?"

The toys sat up with a jerk. They were all alone in the nursery, for Tom and Beryl, whose toys they were, had gone away to stay at their Granny's. The toys were really feeling rather dull. A day at the seaside sounded simply gorgeous!

"How do we go?" asked the pink rabbit.

"By bus," said the goblin grinning. "My bus. I bought it yesterday. Penny each all the way there."

"Ooooh!" said the sailor doll, longingly. "I *would* like to see the sea. I've never been there – and it's dreadful to be a sailor doll and not to know what the sea is like, really it is!"

"Come on, then," said Peeko. "Climb out of the window, all of you. There's plenty of room in the bus."

So the pink rabbit, the sailor doll, the yellow duck, the walking doll, the black dog, and the blue teddy bear all climbed out of the window and got into the goblin's bus, which was standing on the path outside. The goblin took the wheel. The bus gave a roar and a jolt that sent the pink rabbit nearly through the roof – and it was off! It was a fine journey to the sea. The goblin knew all the shortest cuts. It wasn't long before the sailor doll gave a yell and cried, "The sea! The sea!"

"Pooh!" said the goblin. "That's just a duck-pond."

"But aren't those gulls sailing on it?" asked the doll.

"No, *ducks*!" said Peeko.

"Quack, quack!" said the yellow toy duck, and laughed loudly at the sailor doll. After that the doll didn't say anything at all, not even when they came to the real sea and saw it glittering and shining in the sun. He was afraid it might be a duck-pond too – or an extra big puddle!

They all tumbled out of the bus and ran on to the beach. "I'm off for a swim!" said the yellow duck.

"I'd like a sail in a boat!" said the sailor doll. "Oh! There's a nice little boat over there, just my size."

It belonged to a little boy. He had gone home to dinner and had forgotten to take his boat with him. The sailor doll ran to it, pushed it out on to the sea, jumped aboard and was soon enjoying himself!

The pink rabbit thought he would like to make himself a burrow in the sand. It was always difficult to dig a burrow in the nursery. Now he really would be able to dig, and showered sand all over the blue teddy bear.

"Hi, hi, pink rabbit, what are you doing?" cried the bear. But the pink rabbit was already deep in the sandy tunnel, enjoying himself thoroughly, and didn't hear the bear's shout.

"I shall have a nap," said the blue teddy bear. "Don't disturb me, anybody."

He lay down on the soft yellow sand and shut his eyes. Soon a deep growly snore was heard. The black dog giggled and looked at the walking-doll. "Shall we bury him in sand?" he wuffed. "He would be so surprised when he woke up and found himself a sandy bear."

"Yes, let's" said the doll. So they began to bury the sleeping teddy bear in the sand. They piled it over his legs, they piled it over his fat little tummy, they piled it over his arms.

They didn't put any on his head, so all that could be seen of the bear was just his blunt blue snout sticking up. He did look funny.

"I'm off for a walk," said the walking-doll. "This beach is a good place to stretch my legs. I never can walk very far in the nursery – only round and round and round."

She set off over the beach, her long legs twinkling in and out. The black dog was alone. What should he do?

"The sailor doll is sailing. The yellow duck is swimming. The pink rabbit is burrowing. The teddy bear is sleeping. The walking-doll is walking. I think I will go and sniff round for a big fat bone," said the black dog. So off he went.

Now when Peeko the goblin came on the beach two or three hours later, to tell the toys that it was time to go home, do you think he could see a single one? No! There didn't seem to be anyone in sight at all! Peeko was annoyed.

"Just like them to disappear when it's time to go home," he said crossly. "Well, I suppose I must just wait for them, that's all. I'll sit down.

Peeko looked for a nice place to sit. He saw a soft-looking humpy bit of sand. It was really the teddy bear's tummy, buried in the sand, but he didn't know that. He walked over to the humpy bit and sat down in the middle of it.

The blue bear woke up with a jump.

"Oooourrrrrrr," he growled, and sat up suddenly. The goblin fell over in fright. The bear snapped at him and growled again. Then saw it was Peeko.

"What do you mean by sitting down in the middle of me like that?" he said crossly.

"How should I know it was the middle of you when you were all buried in sand?" said Peeko.

"I wasn't," said the bear, in surprise, for he had no idea he had been buried.

"You were," said Peeko.

"I wasn't," said the bear.

"Well, we can go on was-ing and wasn't-ing for ages," said Peeko. Just tell me this, Teddy – where in the world has everyone gone to? It's time to go home."

"Is it really?" said the bear, astonished. "Dear me, it seems as if we've only just come!"

"I don't see why you wanted to come at all if all you do is snore," said Peeko. "Waste of a penny, I call it!"

"Well, if you think that, I won't give you my penny," said the teddy, at once.

"Don't be silly," said the goblin. "Look here, bear, if we don't start soon it will be too late. What am I to do? I'd better go without you."

"Oh no, don't do that," said the bear in alarm. "I'll soon get the others back. We have a special whistle that we use when it's time to go home."

He pursed up his teddy bear mouth and whistled. It was a shrill, loud whistle, and every one of the toys heard it. You should have seen them rushing back to the beach!

The sailor doll sailed his ship proudly to shore, jumped out, and pulled the ship onto the sand. He really did feel a sailor now!

The yellow duck came quacking and swimming in, bobbing up and down in delight. She waddled up the beach, and shook her feathers, sending a shower of drops all over Peeko, who was most annoyed.

The walking-doll tore back across the

beach. The black dog came running up carrying an enormous bone in his mouth, very old and smelly. The toys looked at it in disgust.

"Where's the pink rabbit?" asked Peeko. "He *would* be last!"

The toys giggled. Peeko was standing at the entrance of the pink rabbit's burrow, but he didn't know he was! The toys knew what would happen – and it did!

The pink rabbit had heard the bear's whistling. He was coming back along his burrow. He suddenly shot out, all legs and

sand – and Peeko felt his legs bumped hard, and he sat down very suddenly! The pink rabbit had come out in a great hurry, just between the goblin's legs. The toys laughed till they cried. Peeko was quite angry.

"First I sit on a hump that isn't a hump and get a dreadful fright!" he said. "And then I get bowled over by a silly rabbit who comes out of the sand. Get into the bus all of you, before I say I won't take you home."

They all got into the bus. Most of them were tired and sleepy now, all except the teddy bear, who was very lively indeed – but then, he had been asleep all the time!

They climbed in at the nursery window. They each gave Peeko a penny, and he drove his bus away quietly, and parked it under the lilac bush. The toys crept into the cupboard and sat as still as could be.

And when Tom and Beryl came back the next day from their Granny's they were surprised to see how well and brown their toys all looked.

"Just as if they had been to the sea!" said Tom.

"Don't be silly, Tom!" said Beryl. But he wasn't silly! They *had* been to the sea!

Muzzling the Cat

Once upon a time there lived a big grey cat with orange eyes. He was called Smoky because his fur was the colour of grey smoke. He used to lie on the sunny wall and watch the birds flying about in the trees.

The birds hated Smoky because he was so clever at catching them. He caught their young ones, too, and that made them very miserable. "Let's have a meeting about Smoky," said the thrushes and blackbirds. "Perhaps we can think of some way of stopping his dreadful deeds."

"Friends," said the big blackbird, opening his beautiful orange beak, "we have met here to-day to talk about that horrid cat, Smoky."

At once there was a great deal of twittering and chattering.

"Silence," said the speckled thrush, lifting up one of his feet. Everyone was quiet.

"Smoky catches us and our young ones in a very cruel way," went on the blackbird. "We must stop him. How shall we do this? Has anyone any good ideas?"

So they called a meeting. The robin came, full of woe because one of his youngsters had been caught by Smoky the day before. The wren came, cocking up his perky little tail. The chaffinch came with his pretty salmon-pink breast, and the starling, flashing blue and green in the sunshine. The sparrow was there, too, cheeky as usual, as talkative as the starling.

"Let's all fly round and peck him hard," said the robin, fiercely.

"Well – that would only make him angrier still the next day," said the blackbird. "He would probably kill us all!"

"Let's upset his dish of milk each morning!" cried the wren.

"That's no good!" said the blackbird. "He would be so hungry that he would catch us all the more!"

There was silence for a moment – and then the sparrow and the starling both spoke at once. "Let's-let's-let's…" Then they stopped and glared at one another. They opened their beaks once more. "Let's… let's…"

The starling pecked the sparrow. "Will you be quiet and let *me* speak?" he shouted.

The sparrow pecked at the starling. "You let *me* speak!" he answered back sharply.

"Order, order!" said the thrush sharply. "No quarrelling here!"

"My idea is very good," said the starling hurriedly. "Why not MUZZLE the cat?"

"That was my idea, too!" cried the sparrow in a rage. "I was going to say EXACTLY the same thing!"

"You see," said the starling, taking no notice of the sparrow, "if the cat wears a muzzle, it cannot eat us! There is an old dog's muzzle hanging in the garden shed. We could get that and muzzle the cat well with it."

"A splendid idea," said the blackbird. "Yes, the cat shall be muzzled."

"I thought of it first!" chirrupped the sparrow angrily, trying to peck a feather from the starling's wing.

"You're a story-teller!" squawked the starling. "It was *my* idea!"

"Who is going to do the muzzling?" asked the thrush.

Nobody answered. Nobody wanted *that* little piece of work.

"Come, come," said the blackbird, "*some*body must do it."

"Well, I think it ought to be the one who thought of the idea first," said the thrush firmly.

The starling nearly fell off the tree with fright. The sparrow hid his head under his wing, hoping that nobody would notice he was still there.

"Er… er…" said the starling, at last.

"Well… as the sparrow kept saying just now – it was really *his* idea, not mine. I ought not to have spoken."

The sparrow took his head from beneath his wing in a temper.

"Ho!" he said, "You say it was *my* idea, now you think you've got to muzzle the cat yourself! Well… you can *have* the idea! I don't want it! You said it was yours, and so it is!"

"No quarrelling here!" said the blackbird. "*Both* of you shall do the muzzling together! Sparrow, go and fetch the muzzle from the garden shed."

Off flew the sparrow, and came back with the little wire muzzle in his beak. His smart little mind had thought of an idea to trick the starling.

"Come on, starling!" he cried. "It's no use putting it off. It's got to be done. I'm not a coward, if you are!"

The starling shivered with fright.

"Look," said the sparrow, "I've got the muzzle ready – but I can't muzzle the cat by myself, starling. You must go and hold him still whilst I put it on. Come on!"
The starling gave a great splutter of fright. Hold that cat still! Oooooh!
The very thought made the starling feel quite faint.

"Do hurry up!" chirruped the sparrow. "Smoky is lying on the wall. Just fly down and hold him tightly by the neck. Then, as soon as he is quite still, I will slip the muzzle over his mouth."

"Yes, hurry and help the sparrow!" cried all the other birds to the frightened starling.

But he didn't dare to. He spread his wings and flew squawking and spluttering away, leaving the sparrow and the muzzle behind him.

"Coward! Coward!" cried all the birds.

The sparrow was delighted. "Come along, somebody," he cried. "I don't mind who holds the cat still for me. Will *you*, blackbird?"

"I've got to go back to see my wife," said the blackbird, in a hurry, and he flew off. And before very long the sparrow was left quite alone, chuckling and chirrupping to himself in delight.

Then he heard a voice from below him that made him tremble with fear.

"Ho, little sparrow, I heard all that has been said," said Smoky the cat, with a laugh. "How cowardly all the birds are except you, aren't they? Well, you shall show them how brave you are! I promise to keep quite still, and you shall try to muzzle me. So come down and do what you want to!"

But alas! The sparrow had fled! The muzzle had dropped down to the ground, and Smoky yawned widely showing his sharp white teeth.

"A fuss about nothing!" he said. "They are all as cowardly as each other. I shall go and get my bread and milk."

Have you ever heard the starlings talking loudly to one another, or the sparrows twittering in a crowd among the trees? You'll know what they are talking about now… how the cat was NEARLY muzzled – but not quite!

The Ho-Ho Goblins

Once upon a time the Ho-Ho goblins laid a plan. They wanted to catch the Skippetty pixies, but for a long time they hadn't been able even to get near them. Now they had thought of a marvellous idea!

"Listen!" said Snicky, the head goblin. "You know when the pixies sit down to feast, in the middle of their dancing, don't you? Well, they sit on toadstools! And if *we* grow those toadstools we can put a spell in them so that as soon as the pixies sit down on them, they shoot through the earth into our caves below – and we shall have captured them very nicely indeed!"

"A splendid idea!" said the other goblins in delight. "We'll do it!"

"Leave it all to me," said Snicky. "I will go to them and offer to grow them toadstools for their dance much more cheaply than anyone else – and I will grow them just over our caves, as I said – then the rest is easy."

So the goblins left it to Snicky. As soon as he heard that the invitations to the party had been sent out, he went knocking at the door of Pinky, one of the chief pixies.

"What do you want?" asked Pinky, opening the door. She did not like the Ho-Ho goblins.

"Dear Madam Pinky," said Snicky, bowing low, "I come to ask you if you will kindly allow me to grow the toadstools for you for your dance."

"How much do you charge?" asked Pinky.

"One gold piece for one hundred toadstools," said Snicky.

"That is very cheap," said Pinky. "We had to pay three gold pieces last time."

"Madam, they will be excellent toadstools, strong and beautiful," said Snicky. "Please let the Ho-Ho goblins do them for you."

"Well, I don't like the goblins, but that's no reason why I shouldn't have their toadstools," said Pinky. "Very well. You shall make them for our dance. We want them in the wood under the oak tree."

"Madam, it is very damp there," said Snicky.

"It would be better to grow them under the birch tree."

Snicky knew quite well that under the birch tree lay the caves of the Ho-Ho goblins. He must grow the toadstools there, or the goblins would not be able to capture the pixies as they had planned.

"Oh, very well," said Pinky. "It can't make much difference whether the dance is held under the oak or the birch. We want the toadstools on the next full-moon night, Snicky."

Snicky ran off full of glee. He had got what he wanted! He called a meeting of the others, and told them.

"Now," he said, "not one of you must tell a word of this to anyone, for we must keep it a secret. We must get a runaway spell from Witch Grumple, and each toadstool must be rubbed with the spell. Then, at a magic word, all the toadstools, with the pixies on them, will rush away through the ground straight to our caves below."

"Hurrah!" cried the Ho-Ho goblins. "They will be our servants at last."

Snicky went to ask Witch Grumple for the spell. She was not at home. Her servant, a big black cat with green eyes, said that his mistress had gone walking through the fields to collect some dew shining in the new moon.

"I'll go and meet her," said Snicky. So off he went. He found the witch walking by the hedges that ran round the ripening cornfield. She had a dish in which she was collecting the silvery dewdrops.

"Good evening, Witch Grumple," said Snicky. "May I speak secretly with you for a moment?"

"Certainly," said the witch. She looked all around to see that no-one was about. "Come into the corn," she said. "No-one will hear us then. What is it you want?"

"I want a runaway spell," said Snicky.

"What will you give me for it?" asked the witch.

"I'll give you two Skippetty pixies for servants," said Snicky.

"Don't be silly," said Grumple. "You haven't any pixies to give away!"

"I soon shall have, if you let me have the runaway spell," said Snicky.

"Tell me what you are going to do with it," said Grumple.

"No," said Snicky; "someone might hear me,"

"There is no-one to hear you," said Grumple. "Tell me, or I will not let you have the spell."

So Snicky told Grumple exactly what hewas going to do to capture the pixies, and she shook with laughter.

"Splendid!" she said. "I shall be glad to see those stuck-up little pixies punished. Come back with me and I'll give you the spell."

Now all would have gone well with the Ho-Ho goblins' plan – if someone hadn't overheard the secret that Snicky told Grumple. Who heard it? You will never guess.

The corn heard it with its many, many ears! Grumple had quite forgotten that corn has ears. They were ripe ears, too, ready to catch the slightest whisper. They listened to all that Snicky said, and, because they liked the Skippetty pixies, they wanted to warn them. So the next time the wind blew the corn, it whispered its secret to the breeze.

"Shish-a-shish-a-shish-a-shish!" went the corn as the wind blew over it. The wind understood its language and listened in astonishment to the tale the corn told of Snicky's plan. Off it went to the pixies at once.

When Pinky heard of Snicky's plan, she went pale with rage and fear. To think how that horrid, horrid goblin had nearly tricked her! Off she sped to the Fairy King and told him everything. He laughed and said, "Aha! Now we shall be able to play a nice little trick on Snicky himself!"

So, on the night of the dance, all the pixies laughed and talked as if they had no idea of the toadstool trick. The goblins crept around, watching and waiting for the moment when they could send the toadstools rushing down below to their caves.

Suddenly Pinky stopped the dance and said, "Let's play musical chairs for a change! Goblins, come and play with us!"

The Ho-Ho goblins felt flattered that they should be asked to play with the pixies. So they all came running up. Pinky pointed to the toadstools that Snicky had grown for them.

The band began again. Pixies and goblins ran merrily round the toadstools – but every pixie had been warned not to sit down, but to let the goblins take the toadstools. So, when the music stopped, the goblins made a rush for the toadstools and sat heavily down on them meaning to win the game of musical chairs.

As soon as Pinky saw the goblins sitting on the toadstools, she called out a magic word at the top of her voice. Those toadstools sank down through the ground at top speed! You see, Snicky had rubbed them hard with the runaway spell the night before – and Pinky knew the word to set them off!

To the goblins' great fright, the toadstools rushed down to their cave – and there, calmly waiting for them, were the soldiers of the Fairy King. As the toadstools came to rest in the caves, each goblin was surrounded by three soldiers. They were prisoners!

"That was a fine trick you planned, wasn't it?" grinned a soldier. "But not so fine when it's played on yourselves! Come along now, quick march!"

Off the goblins went – and for a whole year they had to work hard for the pixies, to punish them for trying to play such a horrid trick.

And to this day they don't know who gave their secret away

– although people say that if you listen to the corn as it whispers in the wind, you can, if you have sharp ears, hear it telling the wind all about Witch Grumple and Snicky the goblin. I'd love to hear it, wouldn't you?

Poor Captain Puss!

Ronald and Jill were very lucky. In the summer they always went to Cliffsea, where their father had a house almost on the beach. It was such fun to wake up in the morning and hear the waves splashing on the sands not far off.

All the household went to Cliffsea in the summer, even Toby the dog and Patter the kitten! No-one was left behind. Toby liked the sea very much, and Patter loved playing about in the sand.

Next door to the children's house was a smaller one, and two cats and a dog lived there with their mistress. The dog was called Spot, and the cats were called Sooty and Snowball. So you can guess what they were like to look at.

Toby, Patter, Sooty, Snowball, and Spot were soon good friends. Patter the kitten had a fine time with them. They made quite a fuss of her because she was the smallest and youngest.

So she was rather spoilt, and she became vain and boastful. Ronald and Jill spoilt her, too, and said she was just the cleverest kitten they had ever seen.

"See how she runs after my ball!" said Ronald, as Patter raced over the sand to get his ball.

"See how Patter plays with this bit of seaweed!" said Jill. "She fetched it off the rocks for me, Ronald. She *is* a clever kitten! She can do simply anything."

Patter felt very clever indeed. She went about with her head in the air and began to think that the other animals were rather stupid.

But there was one thing she would not do! She wouldn't go paddling and bathing with the children as Toby and Spot did. No – she hated the water. She thought it was simply horrid to get her dainty little feet wet.

Then one day Ronald and Jill bought down a beautiful big ship to the beach. It was a toy one, but was so big that Toby and Spot could almost get into it. Ronald and Jill played happily with it all morning, and sailed it on the rock-pools that were spread all over the beach.

When they went indoors to dinner the five animals crowded round the pretty boat.

"I wish I could sail in it!" said Toby. "I'd love to sail over that pool. I would make a good captain!"

"So would I," said Spot, wagging his tail and sniffing at the boat as it stood half upright in the sand.

"I would make the *best* captain!" said Patter the kitten boastfully. "Ronald and Jill are always saying what a clever kitten I am. I am sure I could sail this ship much better than any of you!"

"Why, Patter, you little story-teller!" cried Snowball. "You know how you hate to get your feet wet! You wouldn't be any good at all at sailing a boat."

"Yes, I should," said Patter crossly. "I know just what to do. You pull that thing there – the tiller, it's called – and the boat goes this way and that. I heard Ronald say so!"

"You don't know anything about it at all," said Sooty scornfully. "You are just showing off as usual!"

"I'm not!" mewed Patter angrily. She jumped into the boat and put her paw on the tiller. "There you are," she said. "This is what makes the boat go!"

The others laughed at her. They were sure that Patter would hate to go sailing really. They ran off and left her. She stared after them crossly, and then she lay down in the boat in the warm sunshine. She wouldn't go and play with the others if they were going to be so horrid to her. No, they could just play by themselves!

Patter shut her eyes, for the sun was very bright. She put her nose on her paws and slept. She didn't hear the sea coming closer and closer. She didn't know the tide was coming in! It crept up to the boat. It shook it a little. But Patter slept on, dreaming of sardines and cream.

Toby, Spot, Sooty and Snowball wondered where Patter was. They couldn't see her curled up in the ship. They thought she had gone indoors in a huff.

"She is getting to be a very foolish little kitten," said Toby. "We must not take so much notice of her."

"It is silly of her to pretend that she would make such a good sailor," said Sooty. "Everyone knows that cats hate the water."

"Well, we won't bother about her any more," said Snowball. "She's just a little silly. Let's lie down behind this shady rock and have a snooze. I'm sleepy."

So they all lay down and slept. They were far away from the tide and were quite safe.

But Patter was anything but safe! The sea was all round the ship now! In another minute it would be floating! A great big wave came splashing up the beach – and the ship floated! There it was, quite upright, floating beautifully!

The rock-pool disappeared. It was now part of the big sea. The ship sailed merrily on it. It bobbed up and down on the waves.

Patter suddenly woke up, and wondered why things bobbed about so. She sat up and saw that she had fallen asleep in the boat – and when she looked over the side, what a shock for her! She was sailing on the sea! Big waves came and went under the boat. The beach was far away!

"Miaow!" wailed Patter. "Miaow! I'm out at sea! I'm afraid! I shall drown!"

But no-one heard her. The sea was making such a noise as the tide came in. Patter forgot how she had boasted about being a good sailor. She forgot that she had boasted she could sail the boat quite well. She just clung on to the side and watched with frightened eyes as the green waves came and went.

Ronald and Jill suddenly remembered that they had left their sailing ship on the beach.

"My goodness! And the tide's coming in!" said Ronald in dismay. "Quick, Jill, we must go and see if our boat is safe!"

They ran from the house to the beach – and then saw the tide was right in. And, far away, on the big waves, floated their beautiful ship, all by itself!

"Look!" cried Jill. "There it is! But there is someone in it. Who is it, Ronald?"

Ronald stared hard. Then he shouted out in surprise: "Why, it's Patter the kitten! Yes, it really is! Look at her in the boat Jill!"

"Oh, the clever thing!" cried Jill, who really thought the kitten was sailing the ship. "Oh, whoever heard of a kitten sailing a boat before? Spot, Toby, come and look at Patter sailing our ship!"

Spot, Toby, Sooty and Snowball awoke in a hurry and ran to see what all the excitement was about. When they saw Patter the kitten out in the boat, rocking up and down on the sea, they could hardly believe their eyes.

"Captain Puss is sailing the boat," said Jill. "Captain Patter Puss! Isn't she clever?"

But Spot didn't think that Patter was as clever as all that. His sharp ears had caught a tiny mew – and that mew was very, very frightened. It wasn't the voice of a bold captain – it was the mew of a terrified kitten!

"I believe she went to sleep in the boat and the tide came and took it away," wuffed Spot to Toby.

"Well, it will do her good to see that she isn't such a marvellous captain after all!" Toby barked back.

"She *would* be silly enough to fall asleep just when the tide was coming in," said Sooty.

"All the same, she's very frightened," said Snowball, who had heard two or three frightened mews.

"Sail the boat to shore, Patter!" shouted Ronald.

"Sail her in! We don't want to lose her!"

But Patter was much too frightened to pay any attention to what was said. She just went on clinging to the side of the boat. She felt very ill, and wished that she was on dry land.

Spot was quite worried. He knew what a little silly Patter really was – but all the same he thought she had been frightened quite enough. What could be done?

"I'll go and fetch her," wuffed Spot, and he plunged into the sea. He swam strongly through the waves, which were now getting quite big, for the wind had blown up in the afternoon. Up and down went Spot, swimming as fast as he could, for he was really rather afraid that the ship might be blown over in the wind – and then what would happen to Patter!

The boat was a good way out. The wind blew the white sails strongly. The waves bobbed it up and down like a cork. Patter was terribly frightened, for once or twice she thought the boat was going over.

And just as Spot got there, the wind gave the sails such a blow that the boat *did* go over! Smack! The sails hit the sea, and the boat lay on its side. Splash! Poor Patter was thrown into the water. She couldn't swim – but Spot was there just in time! He caught hold of her by the skin of her neck and, holding her head above the water, he swam back to the shore. The ship lay far out to sea on its side.

Spot put poor, wet, cold Patter on the sand, and shook himself. Patter mewed weakly.

The others came running up to her,

"Well, you didn't make such a good sailor after all," said Sooty.

"Don't say unkind things now," said Snowball. "Patter has been punished enough. Come into the house, Patter, and sit by the kitchen fire and dry yourself."

Ronald and Jill watched the five animals running into the house. Then Ronald turned up his shorts and went wading into the water to see if he could get back his boat.

"That kitten was silly!" he said. "She took my boat out to sea, couldn't sail it back again, made it flop on to its side, and fell out herself! She isn't so clever as she thinks."

He got back his boat and went to dry the sails in the kitchen. Patter was there, sitting as close to the fire as she could, getting dry.

"Hullo, Captain Puss!" said Ronald. "I don't think you are much of a sailor!"

"No, she is just a dear, silly little kitten," said Jill.

Patter felt ashamed. How she wished she hadn't boasted about being a good sailor! She wondered if the others would ever speak to her again.

They did, of course, and as soon as they found that she wasn't boastful any more they were as good friends as ever.

But if Patter forgets, they laugh and say, "Now, Captain Patter! Would you like to go sailing again?"

Goldie and the Toys

Once there was a canary in a cage. The bird was as yellow as gold, so he was called Goldie. He belonged to Eric and Hilda, and they were very fond of him; they cleaned out his cage every day and gave him fresh food and water.

Now every night he used to watch the toys come alive and play with one another. He would peep out of his cage with his bright black eyes and long to get out and play with the dolls and animals. They had such good times.

"Do open my cage door and let me out!" he would beg each night. "I want to dance with the curly-haired doll! I want to ride in that big train! I want to wind up the musical boxand hear it sing. Oh, do let me out, toys!"

But they wouldn't, for they knew that he might escape out of the nursery, and then Eric and Hilda would be very sad. So they shook their heads and went on playing by themselves.

But one night, after Christmas, there was a new toy in the nursery. This was a green duck, and it liked the look of the yellow canary very much. So when the little bird began to call out to the toys to let it out of its cage, the duck spoke up.

"Why don't we let the canary out to have a bit of fun with us? After all, the poor thing is stuck in its cage all day long and never gets a chance to play a game. I'd like to be friends with it. I'm a bird, too, and I should like a good long chat with another bird."

"Yes, yes!" cried the canary eagerly. "Let me out, duck! I am so lonely up here! I should love a chat with a beautiful bird like you!"

"The windows and the door are shut," said the big doll. "I don't see that it will do any harm. The canary couldn't escape out of the room if it wanted to!"

"I don't want to escape!" cried the canary. "I just want to have a game. I will go back to my cage when everything is over."

"Very well," said the biggest doll. "You shall come out and join us this evening – but remember, if you don't behave properly, we'll never let you out again!"

The canary promised to be good, and the toy clown threw a rope up to the cage, and then climbed right up to it. He opened the door and out flew Goldie, simply delighted to stretch his wings and have a fly round.

You should have seen how Goldie enjoyed himself. The toys set the musical box going and when the tune was tinkled out the canary took hold of the curly-haired doll with his wing and off they danced together over the nursery floor. The canary really danced very well indeed, for he was so light on his feet.

After they had had a good dance, the clockwork train offered to take the toys for a ride. Of course, the canary wanted to drive, and, my goodness me, he drove so fast that the train couldn't see where it was going, and bumped into a chair leg. Out fell all the toys in a heap, and they were not very pleased with the canary. He didn't get bumped at all because as soon as he saw the engine was going to run into the chair leg he simply spread his wings and flew safely into the air!

Then the toys played
hide-and-seek, and the
canary liked that very much
because he could fly up to the top of
the curtains, or on to the clock, and
no toys thought of looking there for him,
so he was the only one that was never
caught. He did enjoy himself.

At last cockcrow came, when all the
toys had to go back to the toy-cupboard
and sleep.

"It's time to go back to your cage,
Goldie," said the big doll; "You've had a
lovely time, haven't you? Just fly back
to your cage now, there's a good bird,
and let the clockwork clown shut
your door."

"Not I!" said Goldie cheekily. "I'm not
going back to my cage for hours and
HOURS and HOURS. No, I'm going to
stay in the nursery and fly about as long
as I like!"

"But you promised!" cried the toys.

"I don't care!" said the naughty canary.

"How dreadful to break a promise!" said the green duck, who was feeling hurt because the canary had hardly spoken a word to him. "I wonder you're not ashamed of yourself. Go back to your cage at once."

But the canary simply wouldn't. He just flew away as soon as any toy came near him. It was most annoying.

"We shall have to do *something*!" said the big doll in despair. "If we leave him loose like this he will fly out of the door in the morning when the housemaid opens it, and then the cat will get him! What *can* we do?"

They all whispered together, and then at last the clockwork clown had an idea.

"Let's spread the table in the dolls' house, and say we're going to have supper there," he said. "The canary will want to join us, of course – and we'll get him in. Then we'll all go out and slam the door. He will have to stay in the dolls' house till morning then."

"Splendid idea!" cried all the toys. They ran to the dolls' house, and began to lay the cloth. They set out the tiny cups, saucers and plates, and then the big doll fetched some sweets from the toy sweet-shop.

"What are you doing?" cried the canary from his perch on a candlestick.

"We're going to have supper," said the clockwork clown.

"Well, I'm coming, too," said the canary.

Down he flew and hopped in at the front door of the dolls' house. The curly-haired doll saw that all the windows were tightly shut, and the clockwork clown stuffed up the chimney with paper so that Goldie couldn't escape that way.

The canary sat down on a chair, and the big doll gave him a sweet on his plate. He

put it into his beak, and didn't notice that one by one all the toys were creeping out of the house. At last he was quite alone.

Slam! The canary jumped up in fright. The door of the dolls' house was tight shut. He was caught.

"Let me out, let me out!" he yelled.

"No," said the toys. "You just stay here!"

"Let me go back to my cage," said the canary.

"No, " said the big doll at once. "As soon as we open the door you would fly away again!"

"I promise I would go back to my cage," said Goldie, pecking the front door with his beak.

"We don't trust you," said the clown. "You broke your promise before, so we are sure you would break it again." Then the toys went to the toy cupboard and fell asleep. The canary hopped on the table of the dolls' house and went to sleep too.

In the morning Eric and Hilda came into the nursery – and the first thing they saw was the open door of the canary's cage. How upset they were!

"Goldie's gone, Goldie's gone!" they cried, "Oh, where can he be?"

Goldie heard his name and he hopped about excitedly in the dolls' house, trilling loudly.

"Listen!" said Eric, astonished. "Can you hear Goldie trilling? Where is he?"

"It sounds as if he were in the dolls' house!" said Hilda, astonished. They knelt down and peeped through the window – and there they saw Goldie, hopping about inside the little house.

"There he is!" said Eric. "But however did he get there? What a funny thing! He can't have got in there and shut the door himself!"

The children opened the door and Eric slipped in his hand and took hold of Goldie very gently – and in two seconds the little canary was safely in his cage once more, singing very loudly indeed.

"I'm sure our big doll is smiling," said Hilda suddenly. "I wonder why?"

"Perhaps she could tell us how Goldie got into the dolls' house!" said Eric.

She certainly could, couldn't she? You may be quite sure that the toys *never* let Goldie out of his cage again. He really was much too naughty to be trusted!

Mrs. Dilly's Duck

Mrs. Dilly had a pet duck. It was large and white and fat, and its name was Jemima. It had a pond all to itself in the garden, and it was very fond of Mrs. Dilly.

One day, when Mrs. Dilly had two friends to tea – Peter Penny and Sally Simple – she told them about her pet duck.

"She's a wonderful creature," she said proudly. "She comes when she's called, and she can shake or nod her head when you ask her questions!"

"Good gracious!" said Peter Penny.

"Call her now," said Sally Simple.

"Jemima, Jemima, Jemima!" cried Mrs. Dilly. The duck was swimming on the pond, but she heard Mrs. Dilly's voice. She swam to the edge, climbed out, waddled down the path and in at the door.

"Quack-quack!" she said.

"Oh, you clever thing," said Peter Penny.

"Do you love your mistress?" said Sally Simple.

Jemima nodded her feathery head twice.

"Do you like worms?" asked Peter Penny.

Jemima nodded her head hard. "Quack, quack, quack!" she said excitedly.

"Would you like to come home with me?" asked Sally Simple.

Jemima shook her head six times. She was much too fond of Mrs. Dilly to want to leave her.

"You're a dear, clever thing!" said Peter Penny, and he held out half of his cake to Jemima. The duck had never tasted cake before and she took it in her beak and gobbled it down eagerly. "Quack" she said, looking up for more. "Quack!"

Sally Simple gave her a bit of bread and butter with raspberry jam on it. Jemima gobbled it up. Ooooh! It was good! Then Mrs. Dilly laughed and held out a ginger biscuit. Jemima gobbled that too. This was better than worms, and better than frogs!

"Now, that's enough," said Mrs. Dilly. "Off you go back to the

pond, Jemima." But the duck didn't want to go. It was nice to be made a fuss of, and how she loved the cake and biscuits and bread and butter! She rubbed her soft head against Peter Penny's knee, and he stroked her.

"Do sell her to me any time you are tired of her," said Peter Penny.

"Or to me," said Sally Simple. "I'd love to have a duck like this!"

Mrs. Dilly shooed Jemima out of the warm kitchen and shut the door. "I don't expect I'd ever want to part with her," she said.

Now Jemima the duck had been so excited over her petting and the titbits she had had, that the next day she thought she would go to the kitchen again and see if there were any more treats to be had. So she left the pond and waddled to the kitchen. The door was open. Jemima went in. Mrs. Dilly had just washed over the floor and it was clean and shining. Jemima's feet were muddy and wet. They left dirty marks all over the floor.

Jemima stood on her toes and looked on the table. There was a cake there, just baked. Jemima took two or three pecks at it. It was very good.

Just then Mrs. Dilly came bustling into the kitchen. When she saw her nice clean floor all marked by Jemima's dirty feet she was very angry. But she was even angrier when she saw her new cake pecked to bits!

"Oh, you naughty duck! Oh, you rascally creature!" she cried, clapping her hands at Jemima and shooing her to the door. "Don't you ever do this again!"

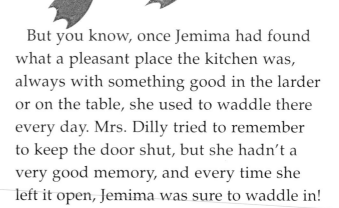

But you know, once Jemima had found what a pleasant place the kitchen was, always with something good in the larder or on the table, she used to waddle there every day. Mrs. Dilly tried to remember to keep the door shut, but she hadn't a very good memory, and every time she left it open, Jemima was sure to waddle in!

The things that naughty duck ate! A string of sausages, a cherry-pie, a pound of chocolate biscuits, and even a large cucumber! Mrs. Dilly got crosser and crosser.

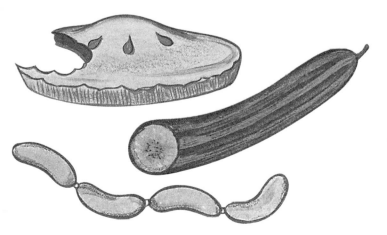

"Now, Jemima, the very next time you come in here, dirtying my kitchen and stealing my food, I shall take you to Peter Penny," she said.

But that afternoon what did she do but leave her door open again, and of course in waddled Jemima and gobbled up a jam tart in the larder!

Mrs. Dilly was very cross. She put on her shawl and hat, tied a string round Jemima's leg, and set off to get the train to Peter Penny's. Jemima was miserable, but she had to go.

Mrs. Dilly took a ticket for herself and one for Jemima. Then she bought a paper and sat down on a seat to wait for the train. She tied Jemima's string to the seat.

Soon, with a roar and a clatter, the train came in. Jemima was frightened and went under the seat. Mrs. Dilly folded her paper, thinking hard about what she had been reading, and ran to the train. She forgot all about Jemima!

She got into the carriage and the train went off. Mrs. Dilly read her paper again. She got out at the next station and set off for Peter Penny's house. Peter was in the garden, working.

"Good-day," he said to Mrs. Dilly.

"What have you come along here for?"

"I've brought my duck for you," said Mrs. Dilly. "She's such a nuisance, dirtying my kitchen and stealing food.

"Oh, good!" said Peter Penny, "Where is she?"

Mrs. Dilly looked round for Jemima – but, of course, she wasn't there! She was still in the station!

"Bless us all!" cried Mrs. Dilly. "I've left her by the station seat. How forgetful I am! I must go back and bring her another day."

Well, when she had journeyed back by train to her own station, there was no duck there! Jemima had got tired of hearing trains thundering in and out of the station and had pecked her string in half. Then she had waddled solemnly home, quacking to herself all the way.

"This is too bad, Jemima, too bad!" cried Mrs. Dilly, almost in tears. She took a broom and swept the surprised duck out of the kitchen. "I'll take you to Peter Penny to-morrow as sure as my name is Dilly."

So the next morning Mrs. Dilly tied the string round Jemima's leg one more and hurried to the station. She did not even sit down on the seat this time, in case she forgot Jemima again. She jumped into the train and Jemima had to go too. The frightened duck crept under the seat and lay there whilst the train rumbled on. She was too afraid even to quack.

When she got back to her garden she had seen that the kitchen door was open as usual. So when Mrs. Dilly arrived back in a flurry, wondering wherever her poor duck had gone to, she found Jemima standing on the kitchen rug, her head tucked into her wing, fast asleep – and the lettuces, tomatoes, and radishes were all missing out of the larder!

door to give up her ticket. Then off she went to Peter Penny's.

But she had forgotten Jemima again. The duck was still hiding under the carriage seat. She did not dare to come out. She stayed there till the engine was shunted to the back of the train, ready to go off home once more, for this station was the last one on the line. The train clattered off. When it stopped at Jemima's own station the duck waddled out from under the seat.

Someone opened the door. Jemima jumped out as the passenger was getting in – what a shock he got to see a large duck struggling by him! Jemima gave an anxious quack and waddled out of the station gate. She set off for home.

As for Mrs. Dilly, she soon arrived at Peter Penny's again. "I've brought Jemima as I promised," she said.

"Good!" said Peter Penny. "Bring her in." But there was no duck there to bring in!

"Lawkamussy, I've left her in the train this time!" said Mrs. Dilly, and she hurried back to the station. But the train had gone, so she had to catch the next, worrying all the time about where Jemima had gone.

Mrs. Dilly nodded her head and slept. When the train drew up at the station the porter put his head in at the window and bawled loudly: "Change here! Change here!"

Mrs. Dilly woke with a jump. She bundled herself out and, rubbing her sleepy eyes, went to the station

But she needn't have worried, for Jemima was safely in the kitchen, gobbling up all the flowers out of the vases. Really, you never knew what the duck was going to eat next!

When Mrs. Dilly got home she was very angry indeed. "I'll take you to Sally Simple's this very afternoon!" she scolded. "I don't like to go to Peter's again, for he will laugh at me – but I'll take you to Sally's and leave you there, as sure as there is butter on bread."

So that afternoon once more Jemima had a string tied to her leg and once more she set off down the road, this time to Sally Simple's. They didn't go by train, because Sally's was not very far away. They went through the park, where the children were playing, Jemima following solemnly, waddling on her flat feet.

Mrs. Dilly's shoe-lace came undone. She stopped near some railings, and tied Jemima's string there. There were other strings tied there too – the strings of kites flying high in the air. It was a windy day and the children in the park had brought out their kites. Once they had them high in the air they had tied the strings safely to the railing, so that the kites might fly high, whilst they went off to play ball.

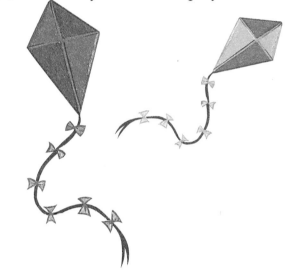

Mrs. Dilly tied up her shoe. Then she untied a string from the railing and set off. But dear old Mrs. Dilly didn't look to see that her string was the right one – and she had untied a kite-string! So off she went, very solemnly, with a kite flying high in the air behind her! How everyone stared!

Sally Simple lived just near the park. Mrs. Dilly went down a street, still flying the kite without knowing it, and knocked at Sally's door.

"Who's there?" cried Sally. "I'm just doing my hair."

"It's Mrs. Dilly," said Mrs. Dilly. "I've brought my bad duck to you. I don't want her anymore."

"Bring her in, then – bring her in," said Sally, and she opened the door, with her hair down her back. How she stared when she saw the kite flying behind Mrs. Dilly.

"Why are you flying a kite?" she asked.

"I'm *not* flying a kite!" said Mrs. Dilly, amazed. She looked round for Jemima – and to her enormous astonishment saw that the string went up into the air!

"It must be that Jemima has flown up high in the sky," she said, pulling at the kite. "It can't be a kite, Sally. It must be Jemima flying up there – and yet she didn't have such a long string."

Sally pulled at the string and the kite came down. "It's a kite, Mrs Dilly," said

Sally. "Well, it's a funny thing that a duck can turn into a kite, but there it is – it seems to have happened!"

Mrs. Dilly was so puzzled that she didn't even remember to say good-bye. She turned and went home, leaving the kite behind her, where it was found by its owner a little while afterwards. Of course Mrs. Dilly didn't find Jemima in the park, for someone had untied the duck and she had waddled home thankfully. When Mrs. Dilly got home she saw Jemima eating the apples out of the fruit dish.

"It seems that I'm not to get rid of you after all, Jemima," said Mrs. Dilly sadly. "I must put up with you. If only I could remember to shut my back door every-thing would be quite all right! Oh – I know what I'll do! I'll get a cat – and then you will be too frightened to come into the kitchen any more!"

So she got a big white cat called Snowy, and it sat in front of the kitchen fire and warmed its toes. At first Jemima was much too scared to come indoors – but do you know what she is doing now? She is making friends with Snowy the cat, and in no time at all she'll be into the kitchen again, gobbling up all the food in the larder – and I shouldn't be surprised if Snowy doesn't help her! Poor Mrs. Dilly! I wonder what she'll do then, don't you?

Off to the Moon!

The pixie Tiptoe was most annoyed with her small servant, Woffles the mouse. He wouldn't do his work, and he had grumbled because there was only bacon rind for his breakfast, and he wanted cheese.

"Woffles, I can't think what is the matter with you," said Tiptoe. "You used to be so happy and hard-working. Now you grumble all day long, and turn up your nose at the nice things I give you to eat."

"I want cheese," said Woffles sulkily.

"But too much cheese isn't good for you," said Tiptoe. "Besides, I can't keep buying the best cheese for you. I don't even have it myself!"

"I shall leave you and go to work for someone else then," said Woffles, taking off his apron and folding it up.

"Who will you work for?" asked Tiptoe.

"I don't know of anyone else who wants a servant. All the fairies and the pixies have their own mice, cats or rabbits."

"I shall go to work for the man in the moon," said Woffles, packing his bag. "I hear the moon is made of green cheese. That will suit me very well. I shall take a nibble of it whenever I like."

Tiptoe began to laugh. "Don't be silly, Woffles," she said. "You will never get to the moon! Stay with me and be a sensible little mouse. I am very fond of you and should miss you if you went!"

But Woffles would not stay. He put on his hat, took up his bag, said good-bye and went. Tiptoe watched him go, shaking her head, for she knew he would never get to the moon.

Woffles wandered here and there, asking his way to the moon, but no-one seemed to know it. They laughed and shook their heads.

"The moon is made of green cheese," said the little mouse. "I am very anxious to go there and work for the man in the moon. He would feed me well, I know!"

Now Tiptoe missed her little mouse, for she was very fond of him. She wondered where he was, and soon found that he was still wandering about, asking the way to the moon. She heard that he was looking thin, for he had had very little to eat. She was sorry for him, but she knew that he would not come back to her until he was sure he could not find the moon. He was a very obstinate little mouse.

So she planned to play a trick on him. She went to her cousin, Pointy, and with much laughter they planned the trick. Her cousin's pointed ears twitched with delight, and he promised to do all that Tiptoe wanted.

He was to buy a green balloon from the toy shop, and blow it up until it was simply enormous. Then he was to hang it on the roof of his house, tied tightly to the chimney so that it looked like the moon in the sky! Woffles would be sure to see it when he came that way, and would think that Pointy was the man in the moon!

Then Pointy would say no, he didn't want a servant, and Woffles would sigh and go back to Tiptoe. It was all very simple!

Pointy bought the balloon and blew it up till it was bigger than he was! He got a ladder and climbed up it with the balloon. He tied it tightly to the chimney – and there it was, shining green in the sky, looking for all the world like the moon!

That day Woffles came along, still carrying his bag, and looking for the man in the moon. When he saw the big balloon away up in the sky he was overjoyed.

"The moon at last!" he cried. "And it is green, too, now that I see it close to! It must be made of cheese after all! I will look for the man who belongs to it, at once!"

He hadn't far to look. Pointy was in the garden, and how he grinned when he saw Woffles coming along.

"I'm so glad to find you," said Woffles. "I have looked for the moon for a long time. I want to be your servant."

"Dear me, I'm really very sorry, but I'm afraid I don't want a servant," said Pointy.

"Oh, but I'm a *very* good one!" said Woffles. "I can cook, bake, sweep, wash, dust, scrub and lay the table. I can–"

"Very nice indeed – but I don't *want* a servant," said Pointy. "You had better go back to where you came from. Jobs are hard to get these days."

Woffles was bitterly disappointed.

"I'm so fond of cheese!" he said. "I thought if I was your servant I could have a nibble of the moon now and then. I know it is made of green cheese."

"Well, that's the first time *I* heard the moon is made of cheese!" said Pointy laughing. "Now go home, little mouse. Go back to your kind mistress."

Woffles turned away sadly. Pointy went indoors, chuckling. Now Tiptoe would soon have her servant back again!

The little mouse looked longingly at the green balloon up in the sky. It did really look like cheese to him, for he had quite made up his mind that it *was* cheese and nothing *but* cheese!

I'll just climb up that ladder, and have a small nibble!" he thought suddenly. "I'm very hungry. I could do with a nice bit of green cheese!"

He put down his bag, ran to the ladder and climbed up it to the roof. He ran up the chimney and then cleverly clung on to the string that the balloon flew from.

He took a bite – and oh, stars and moon and sun! The moon went POP! Yes, it did! It burst to bits and Woffles fell down the chimney right into the pot of cold water that Pointy had just put on to boil! He jumped out, shivering and shaking and Pointy stared at him in great astonishment.

"I bit the moon – and it burst!" stammered poor Woffles. "It's gone! Oh, what shall I do? Oh, why did I leave my darling mistress Tiptoe? Oh, what a fright I got!"

Pointy ran outside and saw the burst balloon on the roof. How he laughed! Poor little mouse, he *must* have got a fright! He ran indoors again.

"Listen, Woffles," he said. "You've spoilt my moon – and as you know now, it *wasn't* made of green cheese – but if you like to go back to Tiptoe, tell her you are sorry for leaving her, and work hard again for her, I'll forgive you and say nothing more about it!"

"Oh, you *are* kind!" wept Woffles, picking up his bag that he had left in the garden. "I'll go back at once. I'll never leave Tiptoe again!"

So back he went, and is with Tiptoe to this very day. When next he saw the moon sailing in the sky, he was very pleased.

"So the man in the moon has got a new moon now!" he said to himself. "I hope nobody bursts it this time!"

Mean Old Mickle

There was once an old farmer who lived all alone in his little thatched cottage. His name was Mickle, and he was mean and selfish.

Mickle had a great deal of money. It was all in gold coins, and he was very fond of it. But he didn't tell anyone about the money – no, he kept it all to himself and didn't spend a penny if he could help it.

His cow gave him milk, his fields gave him corn for bread, his hens gave him eggs, and his sheep gave him wool for clothing. So Mickle grew rich, and each time he sold something for gold he put the gold piece into an old leather bag and hid it away.

He had a good hiding-place. The roof of his cottage was of thick straw thatch, and it was in the thatch that Mickle hid his bag of gold coins.

There was a very good place there, where the straw was thickest, about half-way between the eaves and the top of the roof, and there Mickle pushed his bag of money, drawing the straw over it so that no-one would guess a bag was hidden there.

Often people would ask Mickle for a little help. But always the mean old farmer shook his head.

"I'm poor," he said. "I've not enough for myself. I haven't a penny-piece to give away!"

Sometimes Old Mrs. Handy would come and ask for a shilling or two to help her over a bad time. She had often been good to Mickle, and cleaned out his cottage for him, but Mickle wouldn't help her.

"I'm a poor man," he said to her. "I've nothing to give you, unless you'd like to have two eggs out of the hen's nests for your breakfast."

But even that was not generous of him, for Mickle had already been round all the hen's nests and had taken the eggs for himself.

So Mrs. Hardy didn't find one, and she went without her breakfast.

Mickle liked his cows because they gave him milk, his sheep because they gave him wool, and his hens because they gave him eggs. He liked the pigs, too, but he did not like any other animals or birds.

He kept a dog because Rover barked at any stranger, but the poor dog was tied up all day long, and had hardly anything to eat. He kept a cat because she caught mice, but never did Mickle give the puss a drink of milk or a bite of bread.

As for the wild birds, Mickle hated them all. He threw stones at the sparrows, robbed any nest of young birds, and shouted at all the starlings that perched on his roof to preen their feathers after a bath in the pond.

It was the birds that punished Mickle for his meanness. This is how it happened.

One day a little wren flew down to the thatch of the roof to make a nest there. He pulled the straw this way and that with his beak, and he bit off the ends to make a hole.

And before he had gone very deep into the roof he came to the bag of gold that Mickle had hidden in the thatch!

The wren was an inquisitive little bird who liked to find out everything. The string of the bag was towards him, so he pecked at it. It undid like a long, black worm.

A little mouse ran up the thatch and spoke to the wren. "What have you found? Is it a worm?"

"Help me to pull," said the wren. "There is a bag hidden here. It might be full of food."

So they pulled at the string, but it was tied very tightly round the bag's neck and they could not undo it.

The little mouse had an idea. My teeth are sharp," he said. "I will gnaw at the bag, and then I may perhaps be able to make a hole and get at the food."

So he began to nibble at the bag. He nibbled and gnawed, and gnawed and nibbled, and at last he had made quite a big hole.

He put his nose into the bag and drew it out again. "There's no food there," he said "It's just something round and hard. Good-bye. I'm going to my hole!"

He ran off and left the wren alone. The little bird pecked a bright gold coin out of the bag and looked at it, head on one side.

"I know someone who would like that!" said the wren to himself. "The magpie would! That big black-and-white bird loves anything bright. I'll tell him, and maybe in return he will tell me if he finds any store of insects later in the year, when I have young ones to feed."

So the wren flew off to tell the magpie, who was most interested. The big bird flew back to the roof with the wren. But Mickle, the farmer, saw him and threw a stone at him. It struck the magpie on the tail and a feather fell out.

"I will come back again in the early morning before the farmer is awake!" called the magpie to the wren. So, the next morning, the magpie flew softly down and went to the hole in the thatch with the wren.

He put in his big beak and pulled out a bright coin. My goodness, wasn't he pleased!

"This is a lovely, shiny thing!" he cried, overjoyed. "Just what I love. I will take it to my nest. Are there any more?"

"Heaps!" said the wren, pleased that such a big bird should be so friendly to him. "Take what you want. They cannot be any use if they are left in the roof all the time."

So the magpie told his friends, and soon, in the very early morning, magpies, and jackdaws, too, came flying to get the shining things they loved. Soon there was not a single gold piece in the bag!

And, oh dear, what a shock for Mickle when he next took his bag down from its hiding-place in the roof! He couldn't believe his eyes.

"I've been robbed!" he yelled. "Yes, robbed! Every bit of gold is gone! Help! Police! Help!"

He tore down to the village, with tears streaming down his cheeks. He stopped everyone and told them.

"All my gold is gone! Eighty-seven pieces of it I had, well hidden in the roof! And now it is gone!"

But nobody would believe him. "You said you hadn't a penny-piece," said everyone.

"You said you were a poor man," said Mrs. Handy.

"You're making it up," said the policeman, and he wouldn't even go back to help Mickle look for the lost gold.

Well, it served him right! It is still in the nests of the magpies and the jackdaws, and one day, when those nests fall to pieces in the winter's rain and wind, the bright coins will fall down to the grass below – and, dear me, what a pleasant surprise all the children of the village are going to have!

I do hope you will find one, too!

Smack-Biff-Thud!

Mister Flick lived next door to Dame Tantrum. Flick was hot-tempered and Dame Tantrum was always flying into a rage, so very often there were shouts and yells coming from their gardens.

But for a long time there had been peace. Mister Flick was growing cucumbers in a frame to show at the Fruit and Flower Show in the village, and he was afraid of quarrelling with Dame Tantrum in case she threw rubbish into his garden and broke his frames.

Dame Tantrum was growing tomatoes out of doors, also for the Show, and she didn't want Mister Flick throwing rubbish into *her* garden either, in case it broke her beautiful tomato plants.

"Ha!" said Mister Flick to himself each morning, as he went to look at his long green cucumbers. "Ha! I'm quite sure there are no finer cucumbers in the village! I shall walk off with first prize, that's certain!"

And Dame Tantrum would look lovingly at her fat tomatoes getting red and round, and rub her hands together in delight. "Best tomatoes in the kingdom!" she said to herself. "And all grown in the open air too! I shall get first prize, there's no doubt of it!"

The great Fruit and Flower Show drew nearer. Mister Flick and Dame Tantrum grew excited. They looked at their cucumbers and tomatoes a dozen times a day. Mister Flick gave his cucumbers four canfuls of water each evening. Dame Tantrum gave her tomatoes a canful for each plant. And the green cucumbers and red tomatoes grew and grew and grew.

Now one evening Mister Flick cut a cucumber for his own supper. The same evening Dame Tantrum picked three ripe tomatoes for *her* supper, and they happened to see one another just going up the garden.

"Good evening," said Mister Flick. "Look at this cucumber. Did you ever see such a fine monster?"

"Good evening," said Dame Tantrum. "Look at my tomatoes! I'm sure you have never grown such beauties."

"I don't care for tomatoes," said Mister Flick. "Nasty soft things. Give me a cucumber any time!"

"I've never been able to understand what people see in cucumbers," said Dame Tantrum, offended. "No sweetness, all water and tough flesh!"

"Don't talk nonsense," said Mister Flick.

He held up his fine long curved cucumber and waggled it in front of Dame Tantrum's face. "Look at that for a fine cucumber!"

"Stop waggling the ugly thing under my nose!" cried Dame Tantrum, losing her temper. "It's a silly cucumber. Cucumbers sound silly and they look silly too!"

Mister Flick was angry. He shook the cucumber hard at Dame Tantrum, and, do you know, he shook it so hard that the top end flew off and hit Dame Tantrum on the nose!

Mister Flick was just as surprised as Dame Tantrum. When the old dame had got over her shock she screamed at Mister Flick. "You bad man! Throwing cucumbers at me! Well, I can do some throwing too. Take that!"

And she picked a nice ripe tomato out of her basket and threw it straight at Mister Flick. It hit him in the face, Splosh!

"Oh, oh, my beautiful cucumbers!" cried Mister Flick, looking at three that he had broken in half. "Oh, you bad-tempered old dame! Take my broken cucumbers!"

And Mister Flick began to throw the broken halves of his cucumbers over the wall at Dame Tantrum! Well, really! That was more than she could stand!

"I'm as good a shot as you!" she cried, and she threw her third tomato at Mister Flick. Plonk! It hit his forehead and the red juice dripped down Mister Flick's face. He quite lost his temper then.

"I'll teach you, I'll teach you!" he yelled, and he pulled at all the cucumbers he could see, waggled them hard at Dame Tantrum, and off flew the tops and hit her on the nose! Some people passing by stopped to gaze in surprise, and how they laughed!

"Ooooh!" said Mister Flick, astonished. "Now, Dame Tantrum, stop this! I won't have tomatoes thrown at me!"

"Oh, won't you! Well, have another!" said the cross dame, and she threw a second one at Mister Flick. He tried to dodge it and couldn't, and he fell back into one of his cucumber frames! By good luck the lid was off, so he didn't break any glass, but he sat down heavily on a fine cucumber plant!

Well, Dame Tantrum rushed to her tomato plants and pulled as many tomatoes as she could see. Soon she was pelting Mister Flick with them as if they were snowballs. Splash–thud–smack! And plop–biff! went the cucumbers! It was a sight to see!

Then Mister Plod the village policeman came by, and he was shocked. He went in at Dame Tantrum's garden gate and spoke sternly to the two sillies.

"Stop this at once!" he said. "Whatever do you think you are doing? I thought you were growing these lovely cucumbers and tomatoes for the Show!"

Mister Flick and Dame Tantrum stopped their throwing and stared at Mister Plod. Dame Tantrum suddenly saw dozens of beautiful tomatoes smashed on the ground, and Mister Flick saw his fine cucumbers all in bits!

"Oh, I shan't win any prize now!" they both wailed. And Dame Tantrum burst into tears, and Mister Flick went as red as one of the tomatoes!

"It serves you right," said Mister Plod sternly. "If you can't manage your tempers, you deserve to lose your prize vegetables. Clear up the mess, please."

They spent the evening clearing up the mess. It was dreadful to have to throw the cucumbers and tomatoes on the rubbish heap. Mister Flick saw Dame Tantrum crying, and felt sorry for her.

He poked his head over the wall. "I'm sorry about it all," he said. "Let's be friends. It's too late now to grow cucumbers and tomatoes for the Show this week, but we'll have supper together one night with a salad of young cucumbers and tomatoes!"

So they did – and now they are great friends. They mean to take the first prizes next year, whatever happens.